Pu

BETTER DAVIS
and other stories

Read by Strangers

At Danceteria and Other Stories

BETTER DAVIS
and other stories

Philip Dean Walker

SQUARES & REBELS
Minneapolis, MN

ACKNOWLEDGMENTS

The story "The Line" previously appeared in *A&U Magazine*. It was nominated for a Pushcart Prize.

DISCLAIMER

This is a work of fiction. Names, characters, businesses, places, events, and incidents are either the products of the author's imagination or used in a fictitious manner. Even though celebrities and historical figures may be used as characters in these stories, their actions or dialogue should not be construed as factual or historical truths.

COPYRIGHT

Squares & Rebels
PO Box 3941
Minneapolis, MN 55403-0941
E-mail: squaresandrebels@gmail.com
Online: squaresandrebels.com

Printed in the United States of America.
ISBN: 978-1-941960-15-8
Library of Congress Control Number: 2021937389

A Squares & Rebels First Edition

To the memory of

Dr. Richard McCann (1949-2021)

"Flag of stars! thick-sprinkled bunting!
Long yet your road, fateful flag—long yet your road, and
    lined with bloody death!
For the prize I see at issue, at last is the world!"
                        —Walt Whitman, *Drum-Taps* (1865)

Very Special Episode

Jim watched the television in the waiting room of Dr. Mallory's office while he waited for his test results. Something was playing on a loop on the screen. It was a cheaply shot dramatization of a patient going into a doctor's office to receive his results. It had the feel and quality of one of those local commercials for car dealerships or wall-to-wall carpeting, the ones shoehorned into daytime broadcasts, with bad audio and production value. To Jim, the video seemed meant to prepare patients watching it for what to expect when they got their own results.

He almost couldn't believe it, but the man who was playing the patient in the video had once been in an acting class with Jim when he first moved to L.A. in 1977. It had only been eight years ago, but it felt almost like an entirely different era. The Homosexual Mesozoic Era when he was still a complete nobody and sometimes paid for acting classes instead of food. The pre-plague years—those halcyon days when the worst thing that could happen to him was being stood up on a date, or getting crabs, or having a hot guy bust too soon at Flex on a Friday night. Such little tragedies back then.

Soon after the end of that acting class, Jim had landed a part in a local production of *Godspell* at Hollywood Presbyterian. One night, his performance caught the attention of a casting agent who was in the audience. The next day, the agent recommended him to a director to play a character named Monroe Ficus on an episode of a new ABC sitcom called *Too Close for Comfort*.

He was almost positive that the name of the actor— the one who was playing the patient in his doctor's waiting room video—was Travis. He could remember Travis playing Brick in a *Cat on a Hot Tin Roof* scene in that same acting class opposite a friend of Jim's named Lana who had played Maggie the Cat.

Travis was the kind of man one might have assumed was straight back then, but all the signs had been there for Jim to see that Travis was probably gay or, at the very least, bisexual. He was muscular without looking like Rambo. He had the clone mustache and that little tuft of black chest hair popping out of his Lacoste shirts, the ones that hugged his biceps so perfectly you'd have thought the sleeves had rubber bands built into them. He was spectacularly butch in almost every way that Jim was not. And the way he had played Brick had been so alluring, too. So seductive. It felt like he was taunting Jim at every moment with his huge dick in those silk pajama bottoms he wore in the scene. Like he might just whip it out at any moment.

"How do you know Travis isn't straight? I mean, have you fucked him?" Lana asked one day after their class. She always proudly introduced herself to straight men as "The World's Thinnest Fag Hag."

"No, but I can usually tell," Jim said.

"I dare you to sleep with him then," Lana challenged him.

"I dare *you* to!" said Jim, laughing. "Honestly, I don't think it would be that hard for either of us to get him into bed. He comes across as very *all-purpose*, if you know what I mean."

"No, I don't, actually," said Lana.

"Well, then, you're not a very good fag hag, Lana! See, I know a guy in his early thirties who's as rugged and manly as they come—has a wife and two kids and is, like, a total pussy hound. But he's always had sex with men too, from his teenage years all the way to the present day," Jim said. "*And* he's a total bottom who loves to be rimmed and fucked."

"And I assume you've done the rimming and fucking?" asked Lana.

"Oh, well, I would never tell …" Jim smiled.

But he did eventually tell Lana that, of course, he had rimmed and fucked the married man countless times—Vincent, no last name ever provided. In the parking lot of a hardware store in Van Nuys in Vincent's car with Jim's head bumping into a toddler's car seat; at Flex one night when Vincent had mysteriously shown up, latching himself onto Jim as if Jim were a tour guide ushering him through the bathhouse underworld. Even in Vincent's own house once when his wife and kids were visiting his mother-in-law.

How funny it was to see Travis again after all these years, he thought. And here, of all places. In this hideous waiting room. The absolute last place on Earth Jim wanted to be.

The video looked fairly recent. Travis was a little thinner perhaps, but just as handsome as ever. His mustache had grown into a nice, full beard and he was wearing tight faded jeans so that Jim could still see that package, flopped up against his meaty thigh.

Lana told Jim at est, a couple of years after their acting class, that she herself had once seen Travis in a 1980 episode of *Charlie's Angels* called "Toni's Boys." It was one of those backdoor pilots where the "Charlie" equivalent was being played by an ancient and very slow-moving Barbara Stanwyck who was in charge of three hunky disco dreamboats, one of whom happened to have been played by Travis. None of the guys could act for shit, including Travis, and the planned *Toni's Boys* spin-off never happened.

"Honestly, it looked like they did their casting by sweeping up last call at Numbers!" Lana had told him.

"They should just do a gay porn version where a boozy old madam whores out a gorgeous trio of male hustlers to various johns in Beverly Hills," said Jim.

"Oh, I'd definitely watch that," Lana said.

"Me, too," Jim said.

"You know, someone told me that Travis ended up playing Gooch in an all-male version of *Mame* in La Jolla, but I think they might have been joking. I find that really hard to believe."

"Yikes," Jim said.

It was now painfully clear, watching the video in the doctor's office, that for all of his good looks and the straight-acting leg up, Travis's acting career hadn't really gone anywhere. It was Jim, after all, who had the steady sitcom gig. It was Jim who was about to start taping *Hollywood Squares* as the center square. It was Jim who had some kind of a future in the industry. A future, that is, if he could just stay alive.

There were reasons for Jim to think that his test might very well turn out to be negative. They weren't reasons exactly. They were anecdotes Jim had decided to employ as reasons for his own mental survival.

A man named Omar who went to his gym had been convinced he would test positive. Omar was a financial advisor who had once been the bottom in a gangbang in '82 at the Grove and three of the tops had died in that first wave in West Hollywood. But Omar had tested negative anyway.

"I'm in shock. I mean, I was so convinced that I had it, I was ready to quit my job and cash in my 401k," Omar told Jim while doing bicep curls.

"Are you going to do anything different now that you know you don't have it?" Jim had asked.

"Well, sure. I'll probably use condoms now. But, who knows, maybe I'm immune."

In the video, Travis walked into the doctor's office and sat down across from a man who looked like Martin Balsam wearing a white lab coat and a stethoscope around his neck. Jim couldn't help but laugh out loud when he saw the stethoscope. True, there was nothing funny about any of this, of course, but that stethoscope—it was just sort of ridiculous. So cliché. Every actor needed props. Even Ted Knight had that stupid cow puppet on *Too Close for Comfort*. But there was something so cheap about the stethoscope in Travis's scene. As if a stethoscope was going to save anyone at that point.

The doctor turned his ledger around so that Travis could see the results for himself, matching them with the number he had on a slip of paper. It was bad news. Travis put his hand up to his brow and began to cry, without any tears. Jim felt for his own slip of paper in his pocket. Then Travis looked up at the doctor with a face that had, in the space of a few seconds, become utterly undone and almost broken, pleading for something more. Jim found it unexpectedly haunting. Travis was all of a sudden giving the performance of his life.

"Mr. Bullock?" asked a receptionist. Jim nodded her way. "You can go right in."

He walked into the office and sat down across from Dr. Mallory. He instantly defaulted to what Travis had done in the video: He put both arms on the armrests and sank back in the chair, as if to brace himself for the news.

"So, Jim." Dr. Mallory took off his glasses.

"Where's your fucking stethoscope, doc?"

The security guard waved Jim through the gates at ABC Studios. He went straight to his dressing room—thankfully without running into anyone—and began to leaf through the script for that day's taping.

Jim's character was originally meant to make a single, one-episode appearance in the first season of *Too Close for Comfort*. But he had tested so well with target audiences that the producers decided to make him a permanent member of the cast. He played Monroe Ficus, the foil of the main character, Henry Rush, an exasperated cartoonist played by Ted Knight, who was living with his wife and his two adult daughters who had moved into their parents' basement apartment.

Jim already knew his lines for the episode so he sat back in his chair and looked at himself in the mirror. He tried to locate something, find this new sick version of himself in the same face he'd just seen in his bathroom mirror that morning. But there was no change that he could discern at all. In fact, he somehow looked *more* like himself than he ever had before. He smiled and cocked his head to the side, summoning the bright, cheery, and fey character of Monroe Ficus. Monroe couldn't have *AIDS*. Monroe didn't even have sex. Monroe was a ham! He was funny and harmless! Monroe squeezed easy laughs out of pratfalls!

Jim wanted to say that he felt different now that he knew for sure that he had it. But that's not how he felt at all. Since the disease had first crept up four years ago, he had always just assumed that he would get it at some point. I mean, how could he not? He'd always been too active, too sexual, too trusting, too reckless. Too … *too*. Even in those small moments when he would theorize how he might somehow have evaded it—reviewing encounters from his past in the most minute detail in his mind as if they were sexual Zapruder films, slowing down the screen to look for spilled body fluids, open orifices, spots and sores on penises—it seemed so ridiculous now to have ever thought otherwise. In a way, AIDS had always been his destiny and there was a certain calm now in knowing that here it was. It had finally come for him.

He wondered who could have infected him. It could be anyone. He would probably never know. And that was the rub. Because of that fact, he felt emboldened to choose who he thought it was. Who he thought it should be.

He chose a man he'd gone out with for only several months—Dixon. God, Dixon was so handsome. Smart, funny, instantly charming, with a wonderful smell and the kindest blue eyes. The two had met completely by chance one evening at a party, a small bash held by a mutual acting friend who had recently been nominated for his first Primetime Emmy. Jim and Dixon had been the only ones smoking on the balcony. They began a conversation and Jim could remember just how easy and natural it all was. It really was as if they had known each other for years. Jim was unsure whether or not Dixon was even gay, but halfway through the conversation, Dixon threw in an "ex-boyfriend." He later told Jim that he'd only said that because he knew that Jim couldn't tell.

They went back to Dixon's place in the Hollywood Hills after the party. It was all so beautiful. The house, of course, but also the way that Dixon had held him after they made love. He was the same age as Jim, but was as rich as someone years older.

One night, Dixon whispered "I love you" into Jim's ear, but Jim was too stunned to return the words even though he himself was feeling the same way. No lover had ever said that to him before.

But then Dixon—wonderful, handsome Dixon— just disappeared from Jim's life. Like a ghost. Just. Like. That. He didn't answer any of Jim's phone calls and, if there was an answer, it was his housekeeper and Dixon would never return any of the messages that Jim left with her. Jim had no idea why Dixon had fallen off, and the whole ordeal crushed him in a profound way for months and months afterwards long after he should've gotten over it. Was it because Dixon had become tired of Jim? Was he upset that Jim had misplaced the copy of *The World According to Garp* that Dixon had lent him? Did Jim really actually suck in bed? Or was it because Jim had not said that he loved Dixon too? He didn't know and the not-knowing was like a splinter under his thumbnail. He felt like he was Natalie Wood in *Splendor in the Grass*, the love-struck and doomed Deanie. Like he was going mad.

He would have preferred it if Dixon had just told him to fuck off rather than to disappear like that, without any explanation or reason. Jim liked resolutions and reasons, that was the kind of person he had always been. And this was such an appalling thing to do to someone like him. To withdraw oneself completely. He'd never even considered it. There was a certain level of cruelty that, before this, had simply been beyond Jim's ability to imagine, but one which he was now forced to acknowledge existed.

When Dixon disappeared from his life, Jim dropped into a fuck maze—a months-long marathon of fast food-like sex that left him unsatisfied yet always hungry for more. He spent hours and hours at Flex, fucking anyone who crossed his path, not even seeing their faces in the dark let alone knowing their names. And the virus must have been just marinating around them, dripping like sweat down the black-painted walls, the rough drywall of the backrooms. Circulating through the air. If it wasn't actually Dixon who had given Jim the virus, if he was not technically "the one who did it," well, then it was *because* of him and that was that.

Who knows—maybe Dixon was dead now too just like all the others and it was only Jim's memory of him that would keep Dixon alive now in any sense at all.

That afternoon, they were taping a "very special episode" of *Too Close for Comfort*. On a sitcom, it was one of those episodes that veered off from the usual formula of the show in order to address a current real-world issue such as alcoholism, child abuse, rape, kidnapping, and, nowadays, AIDS. He'd seen a recent episode of *Mr. Belvedere* that had featured Mr. Belvedere's young charge, Wesley, intervening at a Boy Scout camp when the scout leader takes an inappropriate sexual interest in one of Wesley's friends. Jim remembered the episode specifically because once at the Compound baths he had slept with the actor playing the scout leader. The name of the very special episode of *Too Close for Comfort* they were taping was titled "For Every Man, There's Two Women."

It almost seemed like a cruel joke that this was the episode he had to tape that day, today of all the days in his life. The plot synopsis: While working at his job as a college campus security guard, Monroe gets kidnapped by two women in a parking lot and brought back to their apartment where he is tag-team raped throughout the night. Raped by two *women*. Luckily, the rapes would only be described by Monroe to the Rush family and not depicted on-screen. Neil, the director, had sat him down the week before to make sure that he was okay with everything.

"We're not going to do anything that makes you uncomfortable, Jim," Neil stated, emphatically. "That said, I think you have a real opportunity to shine in this episode."

"But is it being played for laughs? Like, 'Ha ha! Look at poor Monroe getting overpowered by women and taken advantage of! It's such a scream!' I'm not even sure how I should be playing this. Am I legitimately traumatized? Is the audience going to be respectful? It's just—"

"Listen, Jim. You've always fed off the energy of the audience. We want you to do that again here. Just like you always have. The audience will decide if this is comedy or tragedy. That's how these type of episodes work. It's usually a little bit of both."

"So I *am* traumatized then?" Jim asked.

"Of course you are. You've just been gang-raped all night! But, like, *Monroe*-traumatized, ya know? It's funny because it's happening to Monroe. Right?" Neil put both of his hands on Jim's shoulders and focused his eyes on him. "Jim, hear me out here. You have always been able to make anything the writers come up with just sing up there. You're a very remarkable person with a very remarkable talent. And don't tell anyone this, especially not Ted, but you're the most popular character on the show. You have the highest Q-rating by far. You're the secret ingredient that makes this whole thing work. Well, you and Cosmic Cow. That's why we decided to write this whole episode for you. Because we have so much faith in you. We know you can sell anything."

"Wouldn't it be more—I don't know—impactful if it were two men who raped me?" Jim asked.

"Oh, God no. That would just be too real," Neil said.

Wearing Monroe's college campus security guard uniform, Jim paced around the set. He felt agitated and unsettled but that seemed to work for his character at the moment. He was slightly disheveled-looking portraying Monroe directly after the attack. Mona, the wardrobe lady, had made his tie askew and ripped one of the pockets on his shirt. She mussed up his hair and then added some hairspray to hold it in place.

"You still look pretty hot for a rape victim, Jim," Mona had said, chuckling.

The other actors in the scene who played the Rush family were already on set and in costume—Ted Knight as Henry Rush, Nancy Dussault as his wife Muriel, Deborah Van Valkenburgh as older daughter

Jackie, and Lydia Cornell as younger sister Sara. The character of Monroe had originally been introduced as a college friend of Sara's but, through the years, Monroe had drifted away from any direct connection with her character at all and now inexplicably worked as a security guard on their college campus.

Jim had never been sexually assaulted himself. But there was a young man who he'd met out in West Hollywood earlier that year named Alex who had revealed to Jim that he'd been raped by his own older brother and had been infected with the virus that way. It was just so cruel and awful to hear, almost unbelievable in its own special kind of horror, that Jim had actively avoided Alex after that. He felt awful about it. He still did, even more so now. But some things were just too horrible to think about, too monstrous to believe, too sad to even look at.

A producer was giving instructions to the live audience. Jim found his mark.

"Are you okay, Jim?" Deborah asked. "You look kind of pale."

"I'm, I'm ... no, I'm about to die, actually. But let's not talk about that now, okay? Fabulous," Jim said. Deborah looked at Lydia with confusion. The two of them both found their marks for the scene.

"Okay, everybody, quiet on set. Now, action!" said Neil. The lights seemed to have gotten brighter. Jim tugged at his tie, dazed. The red light on the camera came on.

They began the scene. Monroe came into the Rush family room in a frenzied state. Jackie and Sara confronted him about what had happened to him. Monroe begged off the question and Jackie asked the rest of the family if any of them knew what was going on. That's when their father, Henry, theorized that the two women who had kidnapped Monroe must have been attracted to him so they decided to take him home and have their way with him.

The audience gave a kind of nervous laughter.

Jackie and Sara were still confused.

"I'm so confused here. A man can't be *raped*," Jackie said.

"Oh, yes, he certainly can be," Henry said.

"Jim, you missed a line there. Monroe is supposed to say 'But that's what happened,'" said the stage manager.

"But that's what happened," Monroe said.

"Okay, we'll just fix that in editing. Next scene, please. Ted and Jim in the kitchen," said Neil.

"What's wrong with you, Jim? You never drop a line," said Ted, running his hands through his thin, white hair. He was wearing a Purdue University sweatshirt.

"Maybe I'm going method, Ted," said Jim.

"What do you mean?" Ted asked.

"Monroe is so struck dumb by what's happened to him that he can't speak properly. Wouldn't that be hilarious? Like Monroe has ever *not* had something to say," Jim said.

Ted looked at him and put his thumb and his forefinger on his chin, stroking a nonexistent beard.

"Neil, give me a second here." Ted pulled Jim aside to the back of the kitchen set. "Jim, I fought against this episode. I thought it was a bad, bad idea. And you can tell from the audience reaction that I was right. Now, I've never really asked you about your life outside of the show. I know you have one. And it's not that I never cared. I just thought it was none of my business."

"Well, it's still not," Jim said.

"I know," Ted said. "And I won't ask any questions about that because it's not been, and never has been, my place. But I've been in this business for a long time, my friend. There's very little I haven't seen or at least heard about. You know, there will always be another job and another script. And another early call. But you. There will only ever be one of you. You're the only 'Jim J. Bullock' we have in stock. I can't imagine anyone else playing Monroe Ficus. And I wouldn't want them here anyway." Ted put his hand on Jim's shoulder and gripped it gently. It was the first time he'd ever touched Jim outside of a scene. Jim nodded his head and smiled.

"Okay, he's ready," Ted told Neil as he found his mark in the kitchen.

"Let's shoot," Neil said.

Ted and Jim both sat down at the kitchen table and began their scene.

The episode title was wrong, Jim thought. For every

man, there weren't two women. There were two men. And two more behind them. Then there were hundreds, maybe thousands, of men behind them. Legions of them. Some faceless, some with no names, some with neither a face nor a name. Some just a memory. For every man, there was another man underneath him, another man behind him, that one in the mirror, carrying the man's truth. For every sick man, there was a healthy man living inside of him. The one who was unblemished, a virgin. For every comic man, there was a tragic man lurking and waiting for his moment to peek out and make himself known. Behind Monroe Ficus, there was Jim J. Bullock. And behind Jim J. Bullock, there was just Jim, a boy looking for a role to play in this great production always teetering toward closing.

Brainstorm

Natalie couldn't have one drink without having *every* drink. Drunk. Wasn't it so wonderful to be drunk? Natalie was drunk. Unreasonably so, for her. But for that moment she never wanted to be anything else.

Natalie couldn't remember if she and Christopher had been sitting at the bar at Doug's Harbor Reef Restaurant for two hours or three when R.J. and Dennis finally met them there. Or was it even four?

She could somehow still sequence the events of the day: The four of them had docked Natalie and R.J.'s pelican blue-colored yacht—*Splendour*—on the Two Harbors side of Catalina in late afternoon and had planned to go for dinner and drinks at Doug's, the only restaurant on that side of the island. But while R.J. and Dennis were both taking naps on the yacht, Natalie and Christopher got bored and decided to take the *Valiant*, *Splendour*'s dinghy, to the restaurant early. They left a note for R.J and Dennis telling them where they'd gone. She and R.J. had named *Splendour* after her most classic film, *Splendor in the Grass*. The *Valiant* was named after R.J.'s portrayal of Prince Valiant in the 1959 film of the same title. A dinghy always trails after a yacht.

Natalie and Christopher had been having drinks at the bar when R.J. and Dennis arrived by water taxi. Natalie was wearing a red quilted jacket over a golden yellow turtleneck sweater and a pair of designer blue jeans. It had been chilly and rainy when they came over on the dinghy so Natalie had kept her jacket on at the bar.

She and Christopher were quite chummy when R.J. and Dennis arrived, laughing and drinking, sharing little private jokes. At one point, Natalie was literally hanging onto Christopher so she wouldn't fall off her stool, she was laughing so hysterically. Even with her back to him, Natalie could feel R.J.'s anger bubbling. Christopher made her laugh. So what? She needed to laugh right now. R.J. could fuck off and she really meant that tonight.

They were all seated in the dining area to eat dinner having finally migrated over from the bar. They had already gone through three wine bottles which now lay empty on the table. A couple nearby who were fans of Natalie's had sent over a fresh bottle of champagne from which they were now all drinking.

Although Natalie was drunk, she was having a small

moment of clarity through the fog of her drunkenness. One of those moments when you come to, awake and alone above the din. She was suddenly drunk enough to realize just how drunk she really was.

"Do you know the rest of your lines, Natalie?" Christopher asked.

"Lines?" she asked, giggling. "Lines of what?" The word could suddenly refer to so many things. Her moment of clarity was over.

"I mean are you off-book? For taping the last scenes of *Brainstorm*," Christopher said. Oh God, of course. *Brainstorm*.

She grabbed her glass of champagne less because she wanted another sip and more to simply steady herself with an action. A prop.

"Natalie has been off-book since before you guys even started filming. She probably knows all of your lines too, Chris. And Louise's and Cliff's," R.J. said to him, clinking his glass with Christopher's. R.J. smiled but Natalie didn't trust it. She knew he wasn't really happy at all.

"I do. I mean, I am," Natalie agreed. "I'm off-book."

"It's such a struggle for me sometimes," Christopher said.

"Well, you have a lot more lines than I do," Natalie said. "I forgot a line during a run-through of *Anastasia* once. It was a dress rehearsal that was open to friends and family, mind you, so it wasn't like it was an empty theater and I could just call out to the stage manager for the line. The whole thing only lasted all of maybe five seconds, but it really seemed to go on a lot longer. And it was terrifying. That has never happened to me before. Luckily, I finally remembered the line but I was scared and embarrassed by the whole thing. I'm sure people could tell."

"I wasn't there," R.J. said. "Lucky for you that you remembered."

"Have you always been so lucky, Natalie?" asked Dennis. Dennis was *Splendour*'s young skipper who had become a good friend of hers and R.J.'s in recent years since they had purchased it. He had basically come with the yacht when they bought it. She loved his straightforwardness and the way he always seemed to want to protect her even if she didn't feel like she needed to be protected.

"No. Honestly, I don't really believe in luck. When I was a little girl, even before I did my first movie, my mother—who we would always call *Mud*, very old-school Russian Mud"—(she delivered as an aside to Christopher)—"Mud used to plant coins for me to find on the sidewalk, always when she thought I wasn't looking. Then I would have to pretend to find them, and then she would say that it was magic. That I was a *magical* person," Natalie said, topping off her champagne. "She seemed to make it her life goal for me to think that about myself. That I was lucky. That I was special. That

I was a magical Russian princess." Natalie paused and took a sip. "I don't think it ever does anyone any good to rely on thinking they're special."

"Well, you are and you know it," said R.J. "You can be a little bitch and you know that too."

"Screw you, R.J.," she said.

"Oh, but *would* you screw me, dear?" R.J. said. "It's been such a long time."

"R.J., come on," said Christopher.

"You can call me Robert, Chris. Only close friends call me R.J. You're Natalie's co-star. You're not a friend," he said.

"R.J.!" said Natalie.

"I don't want to get in the way of your process, dear. Either of your *processes*," R.J. said, adding a very sibilant "s."

However drunk Natalie thought she was, R.J. was drunker. And he was seething. R.J. thought that Natalie and Christopher were having an affair.

Natalie and Christopher were playing estranged spouses in Douglas Trumbull's *Brainstorm*, a science fiction thriller about a device capable of recording the emotions and sensations from one person's brain and transmitting them into another person to experience. R.J. had practically begged Natalie to take the part, yet he had done nothing but complain about it throughout the entire length of filming which was thankfully now almost complete.

Brainstorm would be Natalie's first feature film since the poorly received *The Last Married Couple in America* a year earlier. She didn't know what had gone wrong with that picture but she didn't think it had anything to do with her. The script was middling and her chemistry with George Segal had felt very strained at times.

R.J. and Natalie often invited their co-stars onto *Splendour* like they had done with Christopher that weekend. During the filming of *Last Married Couple*, George, while spending the weekend on their yacht, had made a racist joke that involved Sidney Poitier leaving watermelon seeds between the cushions of the sofa in the main cabin of *Splendour* during his own visit a previous weekend. It had bothered Natalie so much, she could just feel the tension during their interactions for the rest of filming. So maybe the movie flopping really was her fault. She found casual racism and homophobia so ugly, and she always had. She had wanted to punish George for it.

There was no room for any such mistakes on *Brainstorm*. Natalie had to do well in *Brainstorm*. She wanted to continue to bond with Christopher because she felt like it was adding a certain pizzazz to their scenes together. She wasn't an idiot; she'd been in Hollywood since she was four years old. She could see what was happening to her in that town, and it was not good. She was missing out on roles that she should have gotten. Roles for an actress of her age were already scarce.

A perfect example was the Robert Redford situation. Natalie had always considered Bob to be a good friend. Years ago, she had personally chosen him to play the role of her closeted gay husband in *Inside Daisy Clover* which turned out to be his breakthrough performance. However, just last year he had passed on her as the mother in the adaptation of *Ordinary People* he was directing. That was a role that could finally have won her an Oscar.

"I forgot a line in a musical I did once with Liza Minnelli. I just made something up on the spot and the audience went fucking wild for it. Whatshisface even wrote the line I ad-libbed into the book," Christopher said.

"I would have a hard time doing that. Jimmy Dean did that on the set of *Rebel* and I was always so impressed by it." Natalie smiled at Christopher.

"You know, Chris, Natalie decorated *Splendour* from stem to stern. It never looked that good before the Wagners bought it," Dennis said, beaming at her.

"Thank you, Dennis," she said.

"Natalie is really good at *staging* things," R.J. said taking a swig from the cognac he had ordered.

Natalie's friend Mart was supposed to have joined them that weekend but he had canceled at the last minute because of a sick friend. She knew that Mart would have defused the tension at the table. He was always so good with R.J.

"Does your friend have that new disease that gay men are getting?" she had asked Mart.

"I think maybe he does. But no one really knows for sure. You know, there's no test yet." There was a long pause on the phone. "Nat, even *I* could have it."

"Mart, don't even say that," Natalie said. "I wouldn't make it without you."

It was true too, and they both knew it. But Mart wouldn't last long without Natalie either. She had staged an intervention once several years ago to address his excessive drinking and it had worked for some time. Without her there, he would be a mess again in no time. She was sure of that.

"I hope your friend gets better," she said to Mart.

"Yeah. Hope. '*Hope!*'" Mart said. "It's like the title of a bad TV movie I've written. What a mess, you know?"

Mart had started out as Natalie's personal assistant but through the years he had transitioned into a confidant and a close friend. Mart knew everything about Natalie, and Mart was a vault. For instance, he was the only one who knew that R.J. had hit her once and she'd had to run to a neighbor's house for help—to a mother and her fifteen-year-old boy.

When Mart didn't have the funding to mount his play, *The Boys in the Band*, Natalie put it up herself. She hosted a big party for Mart and the cast on opening night.

"People must see this, Mart. No one dies at the

end—it's revolutionary!" she told him when the play had opened.

Natalie had never encountered a film or a play where the gay character was allowed to live at the end. Perhaps not happily (all the characters in Mart's play seemed to be deeply depressed as well as insecure alcoholics), but at least they were alive and breathing when the curtain came down. It had simply never been done.

She remembered Sal Mineo's character in *Rebel Without a Cause*—Plato. It had been so obvious while they were filming that his character was supposed to be gay. And Natalie was pretty sure that both Sal and Jimmy had been playing it that way. Then, of course, Plato was shot dead at the end of the film with Jimmy crying over him. Gays were never allowed to just live.

Natalie and Sal had both received their first Oscar nominations for *Rebel*, but they hadn't spoken in many years. Then she saw him at a film premiere sometime in the mid-seventies. He was with a young man, a blond, almost a Jimmy Dean type. She kissed Sal on the cheek. Then Sal got stabbed to death in West Hollywood a couple weeks later and Natalie was so shaken by it. With Jimmy dead in a car accident in his Spider before *Rebel* even came out and Sal gone now too, she was the only principal from the film left alive. Sometimes it made her feel like she would die in some horrible way too. Finally succumb to her mother's premonition that Natalie would drown in dark water. There was nothing magical about that.

Mart was also the one who had told Natalie a rumor he'd heard about Christopher. Mart said that Christopher had had an affair with the actor who played the "Cowboy" in Mart's play.

"You know, I can almost believe that," Natalie had said. "I bet he was researching a role. He's very method."

But how stupid it was of her to say that. It was the exact same excuse that R.J. had given her years before when she had walked in on *him* and another man when the two of them were married the first time around. It was one lame excuse of several he had offered, none of which she believed. She ended up being the one to take the blame in the press for the end of their marriage in order to save R.J.'s career, but she knew there were still whisperings about it around town. R.J.'s agent back then, Henry Willson, was known to represent closeted gay actors including Rock Hudson and Tab Hunter. She had once overheard at a party that he kept a "stable of faggots." R.J. also had that effeminate butler in the small bachelor pad in Beverly Hills they had moved into back when they were first married. Natalie's mother always found it suspicious that the butler was a live-in in a two-bedroom condo. "Is not normal, Natasha," Mud would say to her. "Makes no sense."

A man with an accordion came over to their table and began playing "Lara's Theme" from *Dr. Zhivago*. It made Natalie think fondly of her Russian parents— her mother's obsession with the Romanov family, her heavy accent, her father's drinking, his handsomeness. Everything that had seemed loud and angry before seemed to pause briefly and she felt drunk enough to let her eyes rest a bit in peace.

"Let's have a toast!" Christopher suggested as the accordion player moved into the center of the restaurant, continuing with the song.

"To what?" asked Dennis.

"To Natalie. To magical Natalie," Christopher said.

"To Natalie," R.J. slurred.

She looked at R.J. and saw him squinting at her. It was the same look he had given her when she had walked in on him with that man. As if she was the one who should watch her step and not the other way around. As if she was the one capable of betrayal.

Maybe R.J. was actually jealous of *her* because of her friendship with Christopher and not the other way around. They had never really discussed his sexuality but now she thought they probably should have at some point.

It was funny after all, this dumb sci-fi movie she and Christopher were in. She wished she could use the device from *Brainstorm* on R.J. She wanted to feel what he really felt about her. About Christopher. About their lives. Record his emotions and feelings onto the device and then press play so she could feel them for herself. There was something so frightening about never really being able to know another person. There was something so frightening about Natalie having married R.J. twice and still not knowing him at all.

But what if she put on the device and there was just a big nothing? A total vacuum. The empty depths of R.J. transformed into the soundtrack of their lives. Like the interminable silence she had experienced when she'd dropped that line in the play. The sound of being alone.

"To splendor in the grass. To glory in the flower," Natalie said. She remembered a toast her father used to say. "*Droozyia! Boodem zdarovy!*" She downed her champagne. Then she stood up and threw the flute against the wall where it smashed against two wooden rowing paddles crisscrossed and covered in fishing net.

"Natalie, what the hell is wrong with you?" R.J. yelled.

"I'm Russian, R.J. This is what Russians *do*," said Natalie.

Elizabeth/Regina

It was any stage actor's worst nightmare: Elizabeth had forgotten her next line. Maureen had just said her line and now it was Elizabeth's turn to say hers. But she had no idea what it was.

The two were on stage playing sisters-in-law in Lillian Hellman's *The Little Foxes* at the Eisenhower Theater at The Kennedy Center in Washington, D.C. as part of a series of out-of-town previews. Elizabeth could tell from the look in Maureen's eyes that Maureen *knew* she didn't know her line. Come on, Liz, she seemed to encourage her. You can do it. Do *her*. Do "Regina."

Playing Regina Hubbard Giddens in *The Little Foxes* marked Elizabeth's stage debut and she'd had to work so hard at memorizing all those lines. Regina has the most out of anyone else in the play. There is hardly a moment when she isn't on the stage. It had been a shocking revelation for Elizabeth even though of course she had known all this before rehearsals began. She knew intellectually that she wouldn't be able to yell "Cut!" and do the scene over again. But here, right in the meat of it, it was so much worse than she could have imagined.

Early on in rehearsals, Elizabeth had found it helpful to use a hook from the line of the character who had the line before hers to trigger her own line. And that had mostly worked. But it didn't work if she couldn't *hear* the line that came before hers which is exactly what had happened tonight. Someone had coughed loudly during Maureen's last line and Elizabeth had missed the tail-end of it completely. So there she was, arrested in a turn-of-the-century living room set, shoveled into a hot beaded garnet gown, looking at Maureen with absolutely nothing to say.

There are ways out of this, Elizabeth thought. She smiled at Maureen in that sly way she had crafted for Regina. She crossed downstage right and busied herself with the crystal decanter at the bar cart. She tipped a little of the liquid into her goblet (unsweetened weak tea that was passing for brandy) and then threw it back.

Elizabeth had suggested to the director that they do a "drunk rehearsal" one day to see what would happen, much to the younger cast members' enthusiasm.

"Elizabeth, we don't have enough insurance on you to cover anything like falling off the stage in a stupor," the director had said.

This was fair. She had a documented history of

walking off sets, demanding extra fees, trashing her dressing rooms, calling in sick, refusing to work for the first two days of her menstruation. It wasn't easy being her and sometimes that job necessitated a day off. But this play was on its way to Broadway and she was a newcomer there. She didn't want to do any of that stuff anymore. It wouldn't be respectful, and she wanted their respect.

Regina Hubbard Giddens was one of *the* great female roles of American theater, a steely no-nonsense Southern bitch who was rich and lethal. For years, Lillian Hellman had not allowed anyone to play her. That is, until Elizabeth's team proposed it as a vehicle for her Broadway debut. They convinced Lillian by telling her how much money the show would make. Anything Elizabeth was attached to made money, even if it was a total piece of shit like *BUtterfield 8*.

Elizabeth was a United States Senator's wife now. And the President and First Lady were in the audience tonight. She was playing the leading lady in a classic play. It was 1981. This was a new decade and Elizabeth would reflect that.

Maureen looked at her in that way she had of so thoroughly inhabiting Birdie, Regina's sister-in-law. But also in an extra new way. Like a person trying to communicate to you that you have food on your chin.

At first, Elizabeth had been annoyed that they were casting Maureen Stapleton. "I said that I wanted to be surrounded by good actors but that not *that* good," she'd said to the producer.

"Maureen is very generous on the stage. She's as good as you've heard, but she doesn't overpower. And, Liz, Regina dominates *The Little Foxes*."

"I don't need to dominate anyone. I'm happy to sit back and learn from others. I've always been a student," Elizabeth said. When she met Maureen, she was instantly attracted to her warmth and humor. Maureen had a mouth on her too and it made Elizabeth love her even more. During previews, Elizabeth asked her all sorts of questions. She wanted to know how to act on stage.

"You have to always be in the moment, ya know? If you don't believe that you are that person on the stage, the audience won't believe it either," Maureen said. "They'll know right away and you'll never get them back."

"But all that applause when I come on the stage and I haven't even delivered a single line yet. They're clapping because I'm 'Elizabeth Taylor.' Not for anything I've even done yet. It's ridiculous."

"You know why they're clapping before you've even said a damn word," Maureen said.

"There's nothing I can do about that," Elizabeth said.

"That's the problem, isn't it? You're thinking too much about the audience, Liz. They're not even really there. I mean, who cares?" Maureen said. "You need to find the parts of Regina that fit into the parts of

Elizabeth. You need to smash the two of you together. You don't have to be either one or the other. You can be both. A little of her and a little of you. You've done it before."

She had. She'd taken her third husband's death so hard that she channeled the grief into the rest of her performance in *Cat on a Hot Tin Roof*. They had been halfway finished with filming at the time of his plane crash and she had yet to tape some of her biggest emotional scenes. It was her strongest work.

"I did a scene with Marilyn Monroe at the Studio once. *Anna Christie*," Maureen said. "I played Marthy— of course. I've been playing older women since I was nineteen. Marilyn was spellbinding as Anna. You couldn't take your eyes off her. Not unlike you, Liz."

"How was she 'spellbinding'?"

"She fought against 'Marilyn' but she never dropped her altogether. She used who she was to make Anna more complete. No one had ever clapped at the Studio after a scene. It simply wasn't done. Except for that one time after our scene. People were falling over themselves clapping for us. I'm not too proud to admit that I liked it."

"Regina is kind of this scorched earth, no holds barred Southern bitch. I have always excelled at playing those," Elizabeth said.

"You have. But don't forget why you've excelled at playing them. Because you believed they were real."

Elizabeth heard another cough in the audience. She looked up and out at them. Just like Maureen told her not to do. But she was in a reverie. She smiled, and held her hand up to her mouth as if Regina had finally confirmed a position inside her head, a furious internal debate now resolved.

Maureen came downstage to pour herself a drink from the same decanter. She whispered the key word from Elizabeth's line to her. And that was all Elizabeth needed.

One of the stagehands was holding a tall glass of vodka that he handed to Maureen the second the cast left the stage after the curtain call. Elizabeth had seen her get those drinks night after night at the end of each show, gulping them down like she was dying of thirst.

"One of the stagehands told me about some place called Pier 9. It's a gay club with drag shows. Come with me?" asked Maureen.

"I love gay bars. I just ditched the Reagans—let's go!" Elizabeth said. "I need a drink."

"Well, you're just in luck. Because we're going where drinks were invented," Maureen said, downing the rest of her vodka.

Elizabeth and Maureen got into a cab and headed to Southwest D.C.

"You saved me today on that stage. That line I

dropped. I blanked out. It was like I had no past, I had no present. There was nothing but that one moment and the moment was terrifying."

"You saved yourself. You're new to the stage. It happens to everyone at some point." Maureen took Elizabeth's hand. "You're really good in this play, Liz. I mean that truly. Isn't it funny that I'm the one playing the old money character? Old frumpy Irish Catholic Maureen. I've always done well playing Jews, Italians, and Irish. Dusty old Southern money, that's something new."

"You drink too much," Liz said. "Why?"

"Why not?" said Maureen. "You marry too much. Why?" she asked.

"Touché."

"I was so drunk one time, I almost drank a candle." Maureen laughed to herself and looked out the window of the cab. "My father fondled me once in a movie theater. That probably has a little something to do with it. Why I drink. But the real answer is simple—I love being drunk. I'd give it all up if I could just be the most beautiful one in the room for one night."

"Let me tell you something about beauty: It's superficial and no one applauds it," Elizabeth said. "By its very nature, it is only skin-deep. You think anyone cared about my acting when I blew up like a whale and had to have costumes completely re-fitted? No, they did not. All they could talk about was my weight gain and how much I didn't look like my old self, as if my actual *self* had ever changed. And how dare they," Elizabeth said. "It's all bunk, Maureen. It's a cameo in a curiosity shop. Beauty is a relic—talent, real talent, like the kind you have—that's forever. Not beauty. Never beauty."

"The only people who can say that are beautiful people," Maureen said.

"I'm so fat now, no one would even believe it's really me," Elizabeth said.

"Oh, they will so. You're more recognizable than the Queen of England."

The cab dropped them off in an industrial, run-down part of the city. The only life around them was coming from the black brick building where Elizabeth could feel a strong beat emanating from the second level.

"Follow me, kid," Maureen said, weaving as she led Elizabeth.

They walked up the stairs and entered a small, grimy anteroom where a very skinny man with pale skin and long black hair tied in a ponytail took their admission fee.

"Nice Liz Taylor drag, honey. Very believable," said the man.

"See, I told you," Maureen said to Elizabeth. "C'mon, let's go get some drinks."

A small stage was surrounded by a half-circle of chairs and small tables. Elizabeth looked out at the crowd on the dance floor. "Call on Me" by Patrice Rushen had come on and the lights started to spin in a kaleidoscope, bathing dancers in splices of red, green, blue, and yellow. "Look out there. Everyone here is really just dancing alone."

"I know," Maureen said. Elizabeth straightened out her dress, a green sparkly shirt-dress that comfortably hid her recent weight gain.

"Let's sit in the back," Elizabeth said.

"No one even knows who I am, Liz. Besides, women are invisible in joints like this. And it's dark as Hades in here anyway."

Maureen placed her handbag at a three-seater and went off to the bar. "I'll go get us some drinky-poos," she said.

Elizabeth looked around at the little cliques of men roaming around in packs. There was often a very confident one flanked by his second and third, very obviously, supporting players. But there were also these loners who floated amidst the packs like satellites. Sometimes it was the most handsome ones who were alone.

She thought about her friend Rock and how he would venture into these bars and clubs to cruise for younger guys. It wasn't fair that he had to live his life like that, lurking in the shadows to find a little companionship. Rock told her that he had aged so much that sometimes he didn't get recognized anymore. What was so bad about that? Elizabeth would love to disappear for a day.

When they were filming *Giant*, she had noticed how combative Rock got with Jimmy Dean who really was a handful back then. She told Rock that they should just "fuck it out."

"I know he's your type," she had told him.

"He's crazy. He's taking over this whole picture. You sleep with crazy and you don't know what you're gonna take home with you," Rock said.

"I got you whiskey straight up," Maureen said, carrying along a tall vodka in a highball for herself.

"Aww, you remembered from Boston," Elizabeth said.

"Of course, I did. I'll remember someone's drink before my own birthday."

The lights dimmed and a skinny man with Dumbo-sized ears and a lime-green tank top took to the microphone at the lip of the small stage.

"I know most of you are here for a performer who really needs no introduction. But for the uninitiated, I would like you to put your filthy little hands together for our resident drag goddess. She puts the green in the corn, the petrified in the forest, and if you tickle her pussy, she'll sing 'I've Written a Letter to Daddy' for you. I give you—the one, the only—Better Davis!"

"Oh my God, how fun!" Maureen said as a man dressed in really quite believable Bette Davis drag flounced onto the stage with a lit cigarette accompanied on either side by two shirtless hunks in sequined runner's shorts.

"Stop clapping for me, you fat fags!" barked Better

Davis. The audience was howling. "I mean, okay. Well, do. Do clap. Clap now. Louder, bitches!"

"Oh, she's divine!" Elizabeth said.

"You know I had dinner with J.C. the other night." Better Davis paused for effect. "No, no, not Jesus Christ. That other needy bitch, Joan Crawford."

The audience laughed again.

"Would you believe that she asked me to set up a play date with her daughter Christina and my daughter B.D.?"

"No! What did you say?" screamed a fat man from the front row who Elizabeth figured for a plant.

"I told her that B.D. really hated Christina but that Christina could come over only if Joan could list—from memory—the 5,000 men she's fucked. And then the 500 animals too. Neeeiiiigh!" Better Davis said into the microphone. "No, but seriously, Joan Crawford would fuck a doorknob if you asked her to."

"Did any of you know that Joan made her stage debut right here in Washington, D.C.? Oh yes, she sure did. She played a maid in *Our American Cousin* right across town at Ford's Theater ... in 1865," Better Davis fanned out her dress and did a curtsy accompanied by a comic rap on a drum backstage.

Maureen whispered to Elizabeth. "I met Joan years ago in New York when she came backstage after a performance of *The Rose Tattoo* and she couldn't have been nicer. I don't believe anything in that book her daughter wrote."

"The gays love this shtick. It doesn't even matter. They love to turn us all into bitches and cunts," Elizabeth said.

Maureen snickered. "Too late—I'm already both!"

"Everyone say hello to my friend Robin over there in the light booth," said Better Davis. A heavyset blonde woman waved to the audience. "You know, Robin is such a fucking slut, the crabs jump *off* her."

"Oh, he's really funny. That's my kind of people right up there," Maureen said. "Look at him, Liz. He knows exactly who he is. And exactly who he isn't. And no one doubts a single thing he's saying. Bette Davis herself would be proud."

"I have to use the ladies' room," Elizabeth said, standing up.

"There is no ladies' room in a gay bar, Liz," said Maureen.

"And who do we have here?" Better Davis said, motioning toward Elizabeth, who was already standing and now standing out. Robin turned the spotlight on her. "I know I'm a hundred years old and have been fucked enough times to have cum dribbling out of my eyeballs, but I swear to God that's Elizabeth Taylor."

"It is!" Maureen yelled, throwing her head back to laugh.

"Irina I Can't Believe It!" Better Davis screamed, losing a hint of Bette.

A true fan, Elizabeth thought kindly.

"Oh, I'd really be so honored if you would join me up here, Miss Taylor. Could you? Would you?"

Elizabeth made her way up to the stage as the fervor of the audience—an audience almost too stunned to comprehend that it was really her—started to grow. She felt that flush again. The applause. The Elizabeth on the outside and the one on the inside, stepping out together under the spotlight.

"Let's do it together, Miss Taylor," the drag queen, Better Davis, said, as she took Elizabeth's hand and gallantly led her to the spot next to her. "Let's do our line. You know the one."

"But I have to *pee*," Elizabeth whispered to the drag queen.

"Drop your undies and just do it right here. We could probably sell it!" Better Davis said.

Some melodramatic music came on, the kind of music that might have played over the opening credits in one of Rock's Douglas Sirk films. Better Davis put her hand on her hip and summoned her best Rosa Moline from *Beyond the Forest*, dashing around the stage. So Elizabeth followed suit, swinging into full Martha mode, mimicking her entrance in *Who's Afraid of Virginia Woolf?* Then they both said the same line together, the one she would never have to try to remember.

"What a *dump!*"

Better Davis

By 1980, Terrence's shows at Pier 9 had become legendary. Hilarious and unique. Bitchy and smart. They were everything truly exceptional about being gay at that time.

Even when Terrence reused material, he would always find some way to transform it into a new experience for the audience. We were friends, but above all else, I counted myself as one of his most devoted fans. And like any true fan, I never missed one of his shows. Not until I moved away, of course, and I'll never forgive myself for missing those shows. Let me tell you this: If you ever saw one of his acts when he performed as his female alter-ego "Better Davis," you can count yourself among the lucky ones. Because there won't be any more shows. I have to bring them all back from memory now.

It starts with a picture of one of Terrence's costumes in my head. Then the other elements materialize around him: the makeup, the music cues, his brilliant Bette Davis cinematic allusions, the wicked camp, his fearless banter with an almost always adoring audience. Memory can be a cruel and crazy thing though. Unreliable most times, strangely insistent on amplifying details you'd much rather forget, coy and acidic even during bouts of nostalgia—whatever nostalgia is. Memory is a comfort but it is also a burn.

Except for Terrence, I had almost no contact with anyone from Washington, D.C. while I was living abroad for three years teaching English to Japanese salarymen in Tokyo. I could always count on my mother for the odd telephone call that was never quite synced up with our prodigious time difference. But the only person with whom I managed to carry on a regular correspondence during that time was Terrence, whose monthly postcards were the highlight of a lonely existence in Japan.

Terrence—God love him—would keep me updated on all the latest affairs, breakups, and D.C. gossip in short, digestible, witty missives—sort of like a gay Dorothy Parker. (Is that an oxymoron? Was she a lez? Well, whatever). He kept me updated on who had dropped out, who had gone back into the closet, who had started hooking, who had beefed up, who had the clap, who was ... well, the list goes on. I still have all the postcards, including the one with a picture of Bette Davis in *Now, Voyager* where he asked if I'd heard of the new gay cancer.

His postcards always featured some gay Hollywood icon: Bette Davis (of course), Joan Crawford, Elizabeth Taylor, Theda Bara, Josephine Baker, Merle Oberon—all those divas we loved back in our happy fag days.

The first postcard I received from him had a photo of Bette Davis in *Of Human Bondage* (in the death throes of tuberculosis) with a Scratch-N-Sniff sticker of a smiling piece of toast with grape jelly slathered on it. "Dear Harrison, Q: How do you separate the men from the boys in Greece? A: With a crowbar." When Natalie Wood drowned, he sent me one with a still of Natalie and Warren Beatty from *Splendor in the Grass* and a simple note on the back: "Oh, Harrison, I'm in deep mourning for our dear Natasha. Do you think Warren cried? Love, T."

By the time I returned to D.C. in late autumn of 1983, AIDS had already begun to ravage the Dupont Circle neighborhood that I knew so well. Terrence had warned me. Sure, there were new bars that hadn't been there when I left (there always are) and new fall faces in the city as there seem to be every year, that annual crop of new college students, government workers, and other assorted faggotry who always repopulated our most transient of cities. However, I could tell that D.C. had also *depopulated*. People were missing. People I had known for years were just gone. People I had slept with. And it wasn't just one or two guys. Whole cliques just weren't there anymore. Entire social circles had evaporated.

Certain underground bars and sex clubs had vanished as well. There used to be a privately run bathhouse off Florida Avenue near 18th Street informally called The Depot. It was right near the Hilton Hotel where Reagan had been shot by John Hinckley while I was still in Tokyo. The Depot had picked up the nickname because of the legendary "trains" that guys would run on willing bottoms there. Back in the day, there would be a refreshment table on the ground level with chips, salsa, beer, and other assorted snacks and then a big tub of Crisco and bottles of poppers on the second floor.

"Can you imagine their hands passing from the bowl of Cheetos to the tub of Crisco to their *assholes* and then *back* to the bowl of Cheetos?" my friend Romeo had asked. He chided me for going to The Depot more times than I liked to admit. "Harrison, they put their hands back in the bowl of Cheetos."

Romeo told me that one night in 1982, a young man had fallen down the stairs at The Depot and broken his neck. Guys had stepped over him for the rest of the night thinking he was just passed out or high or something. It was only when the lights finally came back on that the owner himself discovered that the man had died. His nickname was "Caboose" going along with The Depot's train theme.

"His face was the reason God created paper bags, but he was a very prolific bottom," Romeo said. "He had a hot ass, but he couldn't fuck forever."

The Depot was gone by 1983, and the townhouse in which it had been housed had been renovated into a private home. I witnessed a heterosexual, yuppy couple exiting it together one morning on their way to work. I didn't know if the place had been forcibly condemned after the death of Caboose or if its closure had been tied to the larger, pressing issue of the public health hazard the disease had brought to the community. It might have been abandoned altogether as men even then began to retreat into their plastic worlds of fear elsewhere in the city.

A certain pall had fallen over the District—and not just because the Reagans had taken up residence in my absence. So I went back, back into my memories of my happy fag days.

In one memory, Terrence was performing as Better Davis. During his peak years at Pier 9, there were always renditions of "I've Written a Letter to Daddy" while done up as Baby Jane Hudson spliced with bits of Giorgio Moroder's "Baby Blue" or Terrence *All About Eve*-ing all over the place with a cunty sneer and a lit cigarette in his hand. During those scenes, he would wear an exact replica of the dress Bette Davis is wearing in the "Fasten your seatbelts" party scene (hand-sewn by his best friend, Robin). But Terrence always brought down the house when Better Davis took on the role of Judith Traherne from *Dark Victory*, the rich socialite whose brain tumor has led to a battle with encroaching blindness.

"Where are ya, Ann? I can't see ya, Ann! I think I'm goin' *blind!!!!*" Terrence rasped as Better Davis, crawling all over the stage on his hands and knees, wearing dark sunglasses and waving his arms around like a spastic queen.

"She's over there, Judy!" the audience would scream out on cue. "She's over there!"

In the fall of 1982, right around the time that The Depot shut down, Terrence's postcards stopped arriving to my address in Tokyo. I remember being worried and afraid for him, a feeling I'd never had about him before. Something Terrence would have laughed at.

When I finally got back to the States, I found out from Robin that Terrence had died of AIDS. He never even mentioned that he was sick. When I asked Robin about Terrence's last days, she told me that when he died, he was almost completely blind.

I used to go to a bar called The Frat House. It was located in an old carriage house in an alleyway off P Street in Dupont Circle. When I got back to town, an acquaintance of mine named Richard told me that he'd been casually fucking a bartender who worked there now.

"You should try him, Harrison," Richard said. "His name is Grayson."

When I heard the name Grayson, I had an almost immediate physical reaction. I started to sweat under my arms and I felt my knees give way a little bit. Grayson was the name of the person who had stolen a man named Troy Lovejoy away from me. Grayson was one of the reasons I had left D.C.

It wasn't just one event that had led me to leave. It was a wave of small cruelties that had peaked with one final injustice that I'd found too devastating to ignore. And off I went, booking a ticket to Tokyo practically the next day after Troy ignored me on the street, shutting down my life like the shuttering of a small business, once burgeoning and busy with foot traffic, but that has now fallen into dust and disrepair, no one caring if it ever opened again. Everyone seems to have a breaking point, however the moment of the actual *crack!* always looks different from gay to gay.

When I left town in 1980, the D.C. gays were petty and cruel. If you didn't look a certain way or act a certain way, you were going to have a problem. It was the era of the "Clone" and, suffice it to say, I wasn't one. I tried the look out one summer. I sported a pair of tight denim trousers and a fitted Lacoste shirt and grew my best bushy mustache, and Terrence wasn't having it at all. The first time he saw me in my new look, he screamed like he was in a horror film.

"Hon, what are you doing!?" And then he walked around me like he was my fairy godmother. "This isn't you. No, not at all. Just be you, Harrison. It's the easiest look in the world for you to pull off."

I wasn't even looking to date anyone, but a rare opportunity presented itself one night at Mister P's when an old college buddy of mine introduced me to a well-built, shirtless man named Troy Lovejoy. Troy worked on Capitol Hill as some kind of policy wunderkind, whatever that meant. "The Hill" always sounded to me like such a magical place. It conjured up a shining white edifice built on a mount—solidity, intelligence, access—a truly exalted life. At the time, I was an aspiring poet who mostly waited tables at Annie's on 17th Street and often had trouble paying my rent, so I looked at Troy in a very aspirational way. I got his number and asked him out. We started dating.

Is it okay that I fell in love with Troy's name first before I fell in love with the actual person of Troy? Can I admit that I was that lame? It sounded like a fake name for a fake boyfriend that you pretend you had over the summer. I loved dropping it into conversation with Robin and Terrence.

"*Troy Lovejoy* grew up on a small farm in Michigan but he really was never meant to live that kind of pastoral life. He went to Princeton, you know."

"*Troy Lovejoy* and I sometimes don't speak for days but it's only because I think it makes him want me more."

"*Troy Lovejoy* made love to me all morning and then made us croque monsieurs served on his balcony with mimosas."

While Robin played along, ooo-ing and ahh-ing at appropriate moments, Terrence was instantly suspicious of Troy, taking on the role of a 1940s Miriam Hopkins-style confidante who imparts warnings to the leading lady in drawing rooms with fireplaces.

"Troy Lovejoy? God, he sounds like a gay Tennessee Williams character. *Troy Lovejoy dies offstage while licking an ice cream cone.* Are you sure that's even his real name?"

Terrence had always been a better judge of people than I was, a skill he took full advantage of as a drag queen. He had a kind of noirish instinct about where each person's life was headed. His lack of approval made me very nervous.

"You don't even date, Harrison. Ever. You're a Bathhouse Betty. You once slept with twelve guys in one night," Terrence said.

"It's not that I don't date. It's just that I haven't. So much. In the past."

"*Troy Lovejoy's* cum tastes like honeysuckle nectar and simple syrup!" Terrence said, rolling his eyes and affecting a Bette Davis in *The Little Foxes* accent. "Troy Lovejoy's shits smell like cookies!"

But when you're inside one of those cultish love bubbles, it's very hard to view yourself with any sort of objectivity. Which is what eventually doomed my relationship with Troy Lovejoy.

In late April 1980, four months into our relationship, Romeo invited me and Troy to his birthday dinner at the Tabard Inn on a Saturday night. I had found it immediately odd and unnecessary for Romeo to invite Troy to the dinner. After all, it was only a small gathering that could best be described as a collection of close friends of Romeo's who might or might not already know each other but who were all there to celebrate Romeo. Some instinctual prick in the back of my neck warned me that Troy shouldn't be there. He was not supposed to be there. Troy and Romeo were not even friends.

When Troy and I arrived at the Tabard Inn, a man was sitting alone at a large circular table festooned with streamers and confetti. Troy sat down next to him and I sat down next to Troy. Troy and I both introduced ourselves to the man who said his name was Grayson Greene. He was one of Romeo's friends, someone I did not know but whom I had heard Romeo mention briefly in passing.

When Troy and Grayson shook hands, I saw something happen immediately. It was unmistakable. I don't think I've ever seen the spark between two people like that. It would be too cliché to call it "electric" but it was as if someone had dimmed the lights in the entire restaurant and illuminated the two of them from below with a floor light, casting everyone else in the room as mindless extras who were only there to observe and comment on the two main characters discovering each other as soulmates. *It changed the room*, to put things lightly. And, in my mind, the most obvious thing that had changed was that I had instantly become the invisible man.

Of course, Troy and Grayson ended up having tons of things in common too: They were both from Michigan. They both shared an affinity for some University of Michigan football player, quoting statistics, offering up niche biographical information about him with which they were flirtatiously one-upping each other. I could feel myself slowly sinking into a Plathian depression that could only be solved by taking a dive into the nearest oven.

Their repartee all felt extremely rude and only seemed to momentarily pause once Romeo and the rest of his guests finally began trickling into the restaurant, before starting right back up again for a brand-new audience.

I knew at Romeo's birthday dinner that Troy would eventually leave me for Grayson. There was no truer thing in the world. It was almost as if, after the end of the dinner as we were making our way back to his car, he already had.

I didn't hear from Troy for the next week after the birthday dinner. When this had happened in the past, I would convince myself that he was giving us space, allowing the both of us to yearn for each other more. To lust from afar and then reunite at the moment it felt like we might forget the passion we had last shared. It was really, really stupid. The reason I wasn't hearing from Troy was not something I was ready to confront.

I went alone to Friends, a piano bar at 21st and P

Street, on a Monday night. As soon as I walked in, I saw Troy at the back of the bar and began to make my way to him. Excited to reconnect with him after a week or so of not talking, I was smiling and suddenly felt lighter. As I got closer, however, I spied none other than Grayson standing beside him, both of them laughing and smiling. Troy looked up at me, startled.

"Harrison! This is Grayson Greene. Grayson, Harrison," Troy said.

"We both met him on the same night a week ago, Troy," I said.

"Hello, Harrison. Great to see you again," Grayson said. He went to get some drinks. Grayson was the kind of rival who didn't even know he was your rival which I just found doubly annoying.

"Grayson and I hit it off at Romeo's dinner. And he reminds me of back home," Troy said. "He's just a friend, Harrison."

"A friend with whom you have way more in common than you do me."

"Oh, stop it. Let's just have fun," Troy said. Grayson came back with drinks.

A very scrawny, small, leather-harnessed and capped older man with more missing teeth than actual teeth went up to the piano. With full-throated vigor and without a trace of irony, he sang "What I Did for Love" from *A Chorus Line*.

There was no mistaking it: I had intruded on Troy

and Grayson's first date. I don't even remember what happened the rest of that night, I got so drunk.

A week later, as I was walking down Connecticut Avenue, I saw Troy coming toward me. He spotted me but immediately looked away pretending like he hadn't seen me. Then he quickly rushed across the street to the sidewalk on the opposite side.

And that's when I left town.

So, there was Grayson now working behind the bar at The Frat House three years later.

"Harrison! How's it going? I haven't seen you in years. What can I get you?" Grayson asked.

"Yeah, I just moved back recently. I'll have a whiskey sour." Grayson began to mix the drink, eyeing me while doing it. "How's Troy?" I asked.

"Oh, you haven't heard? Troy died like five months ago."

I did an exaggerated gulp and put my hand up to my chest.

"He broke up with me after a year. I took it pretty hard. After that, he seemed like he was having the time of his life. But then he got sick and, well." I took a sip of my drink and had trouble swallowing it. "He went back to Michigan. He died at his parents' house."

"Oh. Well, I'm sorry," I said. "Really, I am."

"I'm sorry too, Harrison." He looked at me and held the look.

"Thanks. It really doesn't matter now. I don't think

we were ever even a real couple. If it's real, you shouldn't have to put so much effort into it. I pretended to myself that we were more than we really were."

"Troy liked that though. He liked it when the other person had to try harder than him."

"You'd have thought he'd live forever," I said.

Grayson pushed free drinks to me while we caught up on mutual people we knew. I couldn't remember having a better time. Grayson almost made everyone else around us disappear with the strength of his natural sparkle. I could see why Troy had fallen for him.

I went home with him that night and we had sex and we had a lot of it. It was spectacular. Was it revenge in some way? Probably. Who knows. Who cares? It was hot and I wanted him.

Before I left his place in Logan Circle, Grayson made it clear that he was up for it again any time. I was thrilled.

I suggested that we meet up at P Street Beach late night after his shift at The Frat House, thinking that he would never agree to it. But he did. There were several discreet places in the area where men could have sex and I fucked him in each one of them.

Afterwards we sat on the grass like children and talked about nothing. And everything.

"Thank God you pitch *and* catch," I said. "I don't."

"And don't ever change that."

Grayson lit a cigarette.

"So, did Troy just love dating guys who were in the service industry or what?" I asked.

"Ha! I don't know. He was so successful and I don't think he liked competition in that department. At all," Grayson said. "And I'm not destitute, you know!"

"I didn't mean to say you were," I said.

"Oh God, it's fine, Harrison." Grayson locked his leg around mine in the grass. "You see, actually, I came into some money a couple of years ago when my grandfather passed away. Nothing extraordinary but enough to put a down payment on a condo somewhere which is something I've always wanted to do here. I consider D.C. my hometown now, not Lansing."

"That's nice. I wish I had enough money to buy a dinner at 1789! Alas," I said, taking a puff of his cigarette before I gave it back to him.

"An acquaintance of mine named Cleary, who is a realtor, started badgering me about buying a condo. We didn't even know each other that well, but he had somehow overheard me talking to one of my regulars at The Frat House about maybe buying a place and it was like I suddenly became the most important person on Earth to him. He would call me *constantly* suggesting that we go look at condos and townhouses together. I don't even know where he got my number. It was ... a lot."

"Cleary sounds like a vulture," I said.

"Yeah, well, a lot of these gay realtors are here.

It's all very transparent. I mean, I get it. You work on commission and have to hustle. I do the same for tips at the bar. But calm down a little."

"So, what happened with him?" I asked.

"Well, I never did follow through with him and decided to just tuck the cash away and keep paying rent on my place in Logan Circle. Well, last year, I found out about this elaborate Christmas party Cleary had. Like, I think over a hundred people had been invited. He was in the bar around New Year's and I said—half-jokingly, really—that my invitation must've gotten lost in the mail. Which, I know, was aggressive, but it just slipped out. And I did smile after I said it so I thought he would take it as a joke."

"Did he?" I asked.

"No, he did not. It really set him off. He said that he was sorry if I felt 'slighted' in some way. But in this very patronizing tone. He then went on about how many holiday parties he had attended that year and how much travel he had been doing lately and how busy he was. Then—and this was the kicker—he looks me right in the eyes and says, 'I cannot be everything to everyone all the time and for *that* I am sorry.' Can you believe that? Who even talks like that?"

"Oh God," I said. "What a fucking *queen*."

"And then he told me that I should quit smoking! I mean, the balls on him," Grayson said. "He was pretty hot back when he was younger, but he looks like an old worn-out Halston now." Grayson paused for a moment. "I heard that he latches himself onto rich gays with AIDS now. He convinces them to sell their houses to avoid unnecessary taxes when they die. He got one of them to sell his house way under market and then the poor guy ended up dying alone in a hotel room in Southeast!"

"He's not a vulture then. He's a succubus."

"I know. People are so obvious."

"Can I tell you something personal?" I asked.

"You've had my ass every which way possible in this park," Grayson laughed. "So, yes."

"Before you, I hadn't had sex in almost three years," I confessed.

"Why not? You're very good at it," he said.

"There were very few opportunities available for me to have it in Japan. They're weird over there about sex. And I'm not attracted to Asian men."

"It's okay," Grayson said. "You know, if you think about it, the past three years is probably the best time *not* to have had sex in the whole history of the world. This has been a pretty good party for you to miss."

"Like that Christmas party you didn't get invited to?"

"Oh, I always find a way in," Grayson said. "Even if the party's already over."

✳

Robin called me and asked if I would take a walk with her along the Anacostia River in Southwest one day that fall in 1983. She didn't say why but I hoped it was to talk about Terrence. We could talk about anything, I didn't care. But I really hoped it was to talk about Terrence. I needed to talk about him. Everything had changed. Enemies were now lovers. Sex dens were family-friendly townhouses. We had to use rubbers now.

I could use some fresh air.

Robin and I met at the *Titanic* Memorial next to the water. It was a thirteen-foot granite statue of a barrel-chested, god-like man clad in a long robe with his arms outstretched toward the sky. The inscription below him said that the memorial was dedicated to "the men who had given their lives so that women and children could be saved during the *Titanic* disaster."

"Can you believe that shit? What about the *women* who sacrificed themselves for other women? And children? Where's their memorial?" said Robin.

"I don't know. Honestly, I didn't even know this one existed."

"So typical. It's all about the men. Always. Even fucking AIDS," Robin said. "I'm sorry I said that. I didn't mean it."

"It's okay. You're probably not wrong."

"Here, Harrison. Terrence would want you to have these." Robin held out a tin commemorating the wedding of Charles and Diana that had once belonged to Terrence. "They're his ashes."

"Oh. Yeah. Okay, I just didn't know. What about his parents?" I asked.

"They're both dead. His life insurance policy covered cremation, but I never knew what to do with the ashes. They've been sitting on a shelf in my hall closet for the past year and I feel guilty every time I walk by them. You know Terrence would definitely not like to be back in a closet," Robin said. "I'm surprised he's not haunting me about that."

I felt a certain amount of guilt myself. Guilt about not being there when AIDS was taking out whole blocks back home. Japan had had very few cases of the disease while I was there. I had not really thought about it at all. It made me feel ashamed that this thing that had so completely taken over Terrence's life had not even been on my mind when he died. The guilt was embarrassing.

"I wish I could have been here for him, Robin. I feel terrible," I said.

"He went so fast, there wasn't even any time for him to be mad at you for not being there. He knew you had to leave. He knew you had to get away. Maybe you're alive right now because you did."

"I've thought that too," I said.

Robin looked out at the water and I followed her gaze to its target—the Georgetown University crew team gliding by, the small coxswain at the front of the boat barking out commands to the rest of the rowers who were all synchronized in their movements, their strong arms glistening in the sun. I thought of the lifeboats that surrounded the sinking *Titanic*. I read somewhere once that there was a man who had dressed up as a woman trying to fake his way onto a lifeboat. I thought about how large-scale trauma brought out the best and the worst in people.

"Let's throw him into the water. It's so beautiful right here. I think Terrence would have liked us to do it together," I said.

"And then he'd dress up as Better Davis and do a *Hush ... Hush, Sweet Charlotte* number on that ledge over there, wearing a blonde wig and swinging an ax around," Robin said. We both started laughing and then held each other by the edge of the water.

I opened up the tin and pulled out the plastic bag. We grabbed onto it together with both of our hands and tossed Terrence over the railing. The ashes landed in the water at the edge and just sort of sat there, mixing with the oily whorls that shone in the late Sunday sunshine, sloshing up against a cement piling, only briefly leaving a little bit of Terrence caught between land and water.

"You just know he would've hated that," Robin said. "Smeared on a bit of concrete for all eternity like bird shit."

"Possibly, but I think he'd love the crew boys stroking nearby," I said.

"You're right," said Robin. "He would."

"Maybe Terrence really was a better Bette Davis," I said. "Better than the real one, I mean."

Robin leaned in and took my hand. I had started to cry.

"What if the Bette Davis we have now will never be enough?" I asked. "Maybe there's a better way to live."

The Gay Nineties

The plane taxies down the runway before takeoff. Gaëtan is hungover from his typical New York escapades at the Mineshaft the night before. He pulls out a mock seatbelt from the overhead bin next to the forward lavatory. *Safety is important,* he hears the prerecorded voice over the intercom as he, Lila, and Stacey, both of whom are staggered down the aisle in front of him, make the same motions together, clasping and unclasping their belts in unison. *Pull the strap tight in order to secure yourself.*

Just like a leather harness he wore six months ago in San Francisco, he thinks. Those straps. February 1980. A night to remember. He wore it to a Groundhog's Day-themed leather party at the Hothouse baths and banged ten guys, one right after the other, like a row of furry, little dominoes lined up, their asses wagging in the air.

He even got to top a man dressed as "Punxsutawney Phil." Gaëtan the Cat—nine lives and he's only gone through three of them.

The Air Canada flight today is nearly empty. Lila looks back at him and rolls her eyes. "If those fat fucks haven't learned how to buckle an airplane seatbelt at this point in their lives, then they all deserve to die," he remembers her drunkenly crowing over cocktails in Antwerp last month. Lila tosses her buckle onto an empty seat near the center of the plane after the demonstration and then mimes putting on an oxygen mask.

Gaëtan once had a dream that he had survived a plane crash. He was in the water—completely naked—surrounded by burning wreckage, and immediately abandoned all pretense that he was part of the crew, deciding instead to focus on his own survival. A mammoth woman who he had, at first, mistaken for a blow-up flotation device shaped like a whale, drifted by him in the water—inert. He climbed on top of her (the first and only time he can remember straddling a woman for *any* reason—clearly under duress and inside an actual nightmare), hunkered down, and waited for rescue to arrive. At the sound of a loud horn going off in the distance, the fat woman opened her eyes and he woke up in a night sweat—terrified.

He sits in a jump seat and waits for the plane to level off in the air. He has a one-night layover in Minneapolis before working a flight to London tomorrow—from the Big Apple to the Mini Apple. Johnny Appleseed spreading the good love. He has plans to meet up with a handsome pilot named Luke from American Airlines at The Gay 90s tonight. Luke has a warehouse apartment near the club. Gaëtan has been chasing after Luke practically across the globe for months but they've never been able to coordinate their schedules. Has anyone ever looked forward this much to a night in Minneapolis?

"Why is the club named after a decade that hasn't even come yet?" Gaëtan asked Luke on the phone.

"It refers to the 1890s, not the 1990s," Luke said. "Apparently, the 1890s were really great fun."

"C'mon, let's go back there!" Gaëtan said.

Gaëtan tightens the seatbelt strap out of habit and sees, down the front of his shirt, the edge of the newest lesion forming on his chest, eggplant-colored and slightly raised. The last one was on his face near his ear, but he found a doctor in Vancouver to remove it before anyone noticed.

"This kind of skin cancer is very rare, Mr. Dugas. Honestly, I had never seen it before in my life and now you're the third man I've met just this month who has these same lesions. It's very … odd," his doctor told him months ago.

"Just get rid of it. Please. I don't care what it is. I just want it off my damn face. You see, I'm the prettiest one," he said, offering a dim smile. "And I want it gone."

He uses bathhouses now more frequently. They're much more efficient. He can have sex with dozens of men in one location in one night (in a relatively safe and secure environment) rather than spreading out his tricks and endangering himself. He cruised the wrong man a couple months back in Atlanta but luckily he was able to get away without *too* much harm. Bathhouses are dark and Gaëtan doesn't have to explain to his tricks what this or that mark is. Plus, they can't see any marks in the shadows. *Skin cancer is not contagious*, he keeps telling himself. *It is not contagious. I am not contagious.* It has become a mantra for him.

There is an extremely attractive male passenger near the back of the plane. Gaëtan noticed the man when he filed past him and the girls during boarding. Tall, well-built, with thick, dark glasses and a side part. He is very smart-looking, Gaëtan thinks. The man is reading a paperback—*The World According to Garp*. Gaëtan used to be intimidated by smarts in Quebec City when he was growing up. He had always thought his best asset was his face and his ability to charm, not reading books, of which there were always too few in his house. Being an airline steward is the perfect job for him. It allows him to use these assets to great effect. Even while on the clock, he can get a man.

It doesn't take more than a wink and a nod with Sexy Four Eyes. The passenger lifts an eyebrow and smiles in return, watching Gaëtan as he heads toward the lavatory in the back of the plane. Gaëtan has never been turned down for sex. Not once in his entire life. Ever.

Lila has seen this routine before. She gives Gaëtan that mildly chastising look she does, but she smiles too. They have an agreement: She won't say anything about his occasional screw with a passenger in the lavatory and he won't tell her husband about her Mexican abortion.

He leaves the door unlocked and the passenger comes in. No words are exchanged. There's no need for them. Words are for making a case, for convincing. He doesn't have to do that. It's cramped but they have just enough room to start wriggling out of their clothes. The passenger unbuttons his shirt. Gaëtan pulls the man's pants down. He makes a motion to pull Gaëtan's shirt off, but Gaëtan stops him, grabs hold of the man's neck, and redirects his attention to the mirror in front of them. He enters the passenger from behind and watches the man's eyes bulge in the mirror. It's like, if Gaëtan can't watch himself do this, it might never have happened.

"Is it one hundred billion served now?" Lila asks Gaëtan when he meets her in the mess to stock the service cart.

"And counting," says Gaëtan. "He was a Happy Meal."

The Line

Michael sits alone in the front row of the balcony in the empty Shubert Theatre looking down at the line. That thick white line that has been on the stage for seven years now. The line is what you put yourself on not knowing what will happen to you. It's a beginning and an ending.

He can remember being so worried when *A Chorus Line* moved to the Shubert from the Public Theater—the place where it all began. It's such a fragile show; he was afraid that something might get lost in the transfer. That can happen to a new show when it moves to Broadway. He had seen it happen before: Things get lost.

The balcony has always been the best view of the finale of the show. Michael will occasionally watch it from up here, in the dark, in the clouds. The nosebleeds. He is always so proud from way up here. The golden line of them all at the end of the show, drop-kicking in unison, arms linked, smiles plastered across their faces, the revolving periaktos revealing a sunburst as the lights go to black on that never-ending chain of struggling dreamers.

When he first envisioned the staging of the final number, he'd had to venture back. There were so many little bits of his life that he wanted to rearrange into something spectacular and beautiful. First, he went back to the time when he started doing choreography as a child, performing at all those weddings in a little tuxedo that he was always growing out of. He was earning extra money for his family because his father gambled too much. Later, Michael would become a millionaire after the meteoric success of *A Chorus Line*.

But then he had to go back even further. All the way back to watching those old Busby Berkeley movies on a small black-and-white television that sat on top of three yellow phone books on the basement linoleum back in Buffalo. Those huge, wonderful 1930s kaleidoscopic musical numbers of which he could only ever dream of being a part. Shake the kaleidoscope and a new formation would appear. He could imagine the black and white on the television transforming into Technicolor as the chorus line made its way back downstage, colors refracted and redistributed. A whole new panoply of shapes made of bodies. The high kicks. The wide smiles visible even on that little screen. Michael wished he could shake up the world and then arrange the pieces into the order he always wanted.

✳

Michael's cabbie is dressed as Santa Claus and might be a little drunk from the way he's slurring his words. Geraldine Hunt is singing "Can't Fake the Feeling" on the radio.

"You know who I had in this cab last week?" he asks from the front seat.

"I don't know. Mrs. Claus?" Michael asks.

The cabbie gives him a look in the rear-view mirror like, you fucking wise guy. "No. Ann-Margret. You know who she is, right?" The cabbie is very excited recalling his celebrity fare.

"Oh, yes. Of course, I do!" Michael decides to return his excitement. He answers in a voice that is just a little bit queeny and loud. Ann-Margret, after all, *is* very exciting. It's a fact. Michael honestly hasn't thought about her in several years. He and Bobby Avian actually wanted to cast her as Ruth Etting in a musicalization of the film *Love Me or Leave Me*, but the show never got off the ground. He might have envisioned her once as Cassie in *A Chorus Line* when the show first opened. She's too famous though. He doesn't like to have stars playing that role. The show is the star, not any of the performers.

He does a quick bump on the tip of his studio key as they pass Radio City Music Hall.

"Ann-Margret is the best-looking woman I've ever

seen in person. She is a bona fide, goddamn star, I'm tellin' ya," the cabbie says.

"Yes, she is. She's, well, she's *the one*." Michael smirks to himself. He's really never been in awe of stars. He had clashed with Katherine Hepburn during rehearsals for *Coco* because he hadn't treated her like a duchess like everyone else.

Ann-Margret isn't a Cassie. She's more like the unseen star at the end of *A Chorus Line* whom the whole cast is supposed to be dancing around, all time steps and step kicks. Their individuality, so lovingly harnessed during the rest of the show, gets sucked up into this anonymous golden glob receding into the background in service of a leading lady. It's always been such a devastating ending to him.

Ann-Margret is more of a Carlotta in *Follies* now. Maybe he'll direct a revival of that show one day. Another bump in the other nostril. He is feeling the comfort of the drip. It's always like a warm embrace.

The cabbie belches and Michael can definitely smell the whiskey now. People really do drink more during the holidays. He is no exception with the glass of vodka he was nursing and that long white line of coke he Hoovered up before dragging himself out of the Shubert. The holidays have that potent mixture of depression, loneliness, and these endlessly banal parties. Sometimes it's better to just get really fucked up and let yourself go numb. How else are you supposed to get through all of this?

He's on his way to a Christmas costume party for the Shakespeare Festival which is being held in the lobby of the Public Theater, site of the original *A Chorus Line* workshop production and Off-Broadway premiere. The Public is like a church to Michael. And he always feels better at church.

He leans back into the cushion of the cab and feels the pulse of the night accentuated by the lights that streak by the window, the heat of the ghost of Ann-Margret emanating from the backseat, the tingling edges of the blow and the booze catapulting him into this nocturnal fritz.

This is the thing about Ann-Margret: She can do anything that's asked of her on screen *and* she has that one thing that cannot be taught to actors—Star Quality. And she has an enormous amount of it. Michael is convinced he has it too. People are always seeking his approval on their performances, their costumes, their stage presence, every fucking aspect of themselves. It's like they need him to validate that they have it, because intuitively they know that *he* has it.

"I'll be sure to send Ann-Margret your love," Michael says, tossing cash up to the front. "I know her, you know." The cabbie is stunned into silence and Michael flounces out of the cab, laughing.

He shows up to the Public late. The party feels like a dream he should already have had. Isn't there a French word for that? There should be if there isn't already. He dropped out of high school (and French class) to go on tour in *West Side Story* in Paris where all he ever did was speak English so he doesn't know what the French word is for it.

How do all the characters from A Chorus Line *end up anyway?* That's the theme of the party. In the show, the characters are all perpetually stuck in that one moment in time. A person's whole life contained in a one-day audition. But where do each of them end up after the show when they're all old and gray? What happens to them? Does anyone know? And, oh God, what will happen to Michael?

The actors show up to the theater like they've all just been bussed in from a nursing home. They have on the same costumes they wear in the show—those iconic looks designed by Theoni V. Aldredge—but they have dressed themselves up in grey and white old-people wigs and extreme padding for cellulite. They are lumpy and pushing around empty oxygen tanks. It is surreal almost to the point of absurdity. He momentarily feels like he's walking through a sick ward. It's all very *Follies* actually, a bunch of old showgirls showing up for a reunion in a theater about to be demolished.

When Michael first heard the theme of the party, he was annoyed. Why would anyone want to poke fun at these characters by turning them into old people? Cassie's resolve, Sheila's steeliness, Val's versatility, Paul's vulnerability. Do not fuck with these characters. They don't belong to him per se. But they are *his* in a way. They're all *him*. And he feels very protective of them. He could always find himself right up and down that line.

"Oh, Michael, you're finally here!" says Pam who plays the firecracker Val in the current Broadway cast. Her famous tits so comically referenced in "Dance: Ten; Looks: Three" now look like croquet balls swinging around at the end of two long socks attached to her chest. Her tits are literally being dragged on the floor behind her. Tits & Ass. That used to be the name of the song but when the punchline didn't get the laughs, Michael quickly realized that the title of the song was giving away the big joke so he renamed it. Then it got the laughs.

"Pam, your tits are all the way down past your ass!" says Michael. Pam picks them both up off the floor and starts twirling them around while clucking a burlesque beat.

"You'd still hire me though, huh?" she says with a kind of Mae West wink.

"Sparkle, Neely, sparkle!" God, he can be such a little fag.

Bob MacDonald shows up as Zach, who's the one running the audition within the show, a character Michael has always flirted with playing on stage himself. It wouldn't be that much of a stretch if he ever did. Bob uses a walker to heave himself across the threshold.

"Cute, Bob. Very cute," Michael says, eyeing the

walker as it gets caught in some bunched-up carpeting. Bob opens his mouth and a set of dentures falls out onto the floor of the lobby. "Okay! Nice touch!"

"So we're really doing this, I guess, aren't we?" he asks Irene, a lesbian dresser who is watching the parade of characters who have taken over the Public's lobby. She hands him a tall glass of vodka.

"Yep, we sure are. Here, drink up, boss," she says.

"Irene, you've known me for a pretty long time, right?"

"Yeah … ?"

"What would you say is my worst attribute? And pretend that it's not me asking you."

Irene turns away almost stricken, looking anywhere but at his face. "Really?" she says, finally looking at him directly.

"I'm serious. Just tell me."

"Michael, you make people cry," Irene says.

It's true. Michael has made many people cry throughout the years. His shows just have that effect on people. But he knows that's not what Irene means. Michael has made *individuals* cry. On purpose. He used to go into Sammy Williams's dressing room before a show and say to him, "I hate you, Sammy! You're too much of a sissy. You're a little fucking faggot and I just can't fucking stand you anymore." Sammy had the pivotal role of Paul in the original run of the show. Paul, whose long monologue on the line is the emotional high point of the show. Michael had to keep getting Sammy into that dark, vulnerable place right before a show because Sammy wasn't really an actor and he wasn't getting there by himself and that's just how Michael had to do it sometimes. It was all for the good of the show.

"I won it, Michael. I won!" Sammy said to him at the 1976 Tony Awards when Sammy took home the award for Best Featured Actor in a Musical for *A Chorus Line*.

"*I* won it, Sammy. I won it *for* you," Michael responded to him. "I made your entire performance *come*." Sammy looked at him with a mixture of pity and fear.

"Go find us a joint, Irene. I need something to take the edge off," Michael says. He's sort of jumpy and is experiencing that truly awful feeling when the cocaine starts wearing off. Sometimes it feels like the entire decade thus far has just been the manifestation of that exact same feeling. The 1980s: The Decade When the Coke Wore Off.

Irene slinks away in a Blondie T-shirt and army-green parachute pants. Dykes can't dress for shit, he thinks.

He looks up at the stage, that place where it all began. It's different from the Shubert. He can almost see the ghosts of the original cast up there rehearsing. Then the pure magic of opening night. Donna doing her solo dance in the red Cassie dress for the first time, almost like she's doing it just for him. He imagines the long white line drawn at the foot of the stage near the lights. It's a line he can imagine going on forever. The border of an imaginary country that only he and the cast are allowed to live in. A Never-Never Land for theater gypsies. The Orphans of the Chorus.

Michael loves opening night, but he hates opening night reviews. Well, he loves *good* opening night reviews but he hates the idea of being "reviewed" at all. Who the hell was anyone to review him?

He remembers someone telling him that the actress Maureen Stapleton had apparently been appalled by the show. *Appalled*. That was the actual word she had used. She felt that it was unseemly to show actors begging for work. He doesn't think she really understood the universal nature of the show. Everyone can recognize the feeling of placing oneself on the line when they interview for a new job. Constantly debating the question of will I get it or not. Your identity is your job and if you can't do your job, you just don't exist anymore.

He likes Maureen Stapleton. He loved her in *Interiors*. And he was glad when she finally won the Oscar for *Reds* this year. But she just didn't get his show and, knowing her, she was probably blotto during it.

A Chorus Line is not just a musical. It's not just people begging to do what they do best. It's the good and the bad and the laughter and the tears and the shit and the piss and the cum. That's what life is, isn't it? Life is an only vaguely connected series of scenes and interactions with other "players" (your teacher, the guy at the bodega on the corner, your lovers, your *mom*). Life is sex and death, baby.

Life on stage can be just as real as life not on stage. Michael knows that better than anyone. It can be realer, even. And as the director, he can control the way life looks, how life is perceived, the emotions the audience will have. And, hey, if you don't like it, you can get right up out of your plush seat and leave the theater in the middle of the show. No one will stop you. Or you can just wait until intermission and go out there on the street in front of the theater and have a cigarette with the others and then just casually blend back into the hordes of people walking by on the sidewalk, whisking yourself away from those lives that will keep on burning night after night inside on the stage on the line. The people on the street will never know you have just left a musical right in the middle of it. They will never know that, for a couple of hours, you left the world and entered another one. They will let you back into the real world without knowing you had ever left it.

The line between reality and theater is a hazy one for Michael. Which is probably why he's doing so many drugs right now.

Ernie Kraft, a young dancer who was promoted from swing to the role of Bobby a couple of months ago, arrives to the party sporting a pillow paunch stuck under the now-iconic patterned sweater his character wears, a silk scarf tied around his neck like gay Christmas wrapping. Someone has helped him out with a bald cap and a white mustache. Probably Irene.

Ernie missed several performances back-to-back-to-back a couple of weeks ago and Michael has been on the verge of firing him.

"I'm kind of surprised Ernie's even here," says Sebastian who works in the lighting booth. He breathes down Michael's neck from behind. He's very tall.

"Why?" Michael asks.

"He has it."

"What do you mean 'it'?" Michael asks. "It-it? *The* It?"

"*The* It, Michael. The new It," answers Sebastian. "He's an It Boy. GRID or GRAD, the Hot Guy Flu of '82. Whatever the fuck they're calling it today, he has it."

"Fuck. Fuck." Michael pulls out a cigarette. "Shit." Sebastian quickly lights it for him, the flame momentarily lighting up his face. Michael can see Sebastian's square jaw and the way his eyes are kind yet focused.

Michael slept with Sebastian once in the summer of '79. He saw him out while cruising The Piers one night. They had been working together for over four years, but it was almost like he was meeting Sebastian for the first time. Sometimes when you see someone with whom you're already well familiar in a totally different venue, they can seem like a completely different person. Michael used to love that about people. How they could change with just a new angle, a sliver of light shining through a cracked window in a warehouse, while looking up at you from the berth of a confident kneeling position, hands on your fly already zipping it down. And Sebastian is a Beautiful. Blond and masculine and just so very handsome, Michael's favorite type of man. He tends to put guys like Sebastian on a pedestal.

The truth is that Michael thinks of himself as pretty ugly. He's only five-five and has moles all over his face and a patchy, pubic-looking beard. But he has charisma. And charisma can trump ugly. Michael has been able to bed men who were much more attractive than him. And frequently, too. It's an old trick of his and it works beautifully. Star Quality.

But Ernie has It. The It. And Ernie is also one of the Beautifuls. God, everything happens to artists first.

"Ernie, your Bobby got old on me," Michael says, joining him at the refreshments table near the center of the lobby.

"I always heard that Bobby is supposed to be you in the show. Bobby is from Buffalo just like you are after all," Ernie says, ladling light pink punch into a clear plastic cup.

"Who told you that?" Michael asks.

"That line about committing suicide in Buffalo. C'mon, that is *so* you. I love playing you, Michael."

"Bobby isn't me and that line comes from Mark Twain. That's it," Michael says. He shuffles off to join

Irene who is waving a joint in front of her face as an invitation.

It seems unbearably sad to Michael all of a sudden. This boy who will never grow as old as he's dressed himself up as for a costume party. Ernie will never have white hair. Fuck it, Ernie won't even live to see the year 1984. Ernie will probably die before Michael has to change the light bulb in his bedside lamp. Michael starts to imagine who could replace Ernie in the show. One thought naturally follows the other.

"Guess who?" Donna's hands are over his eyes and he can feel the bulge of a belly knocking him in the back. He turns around to discover her wearing a red tailored Cassie dress ballooned out to accommodate a huge belly. She's sporting a frizzy white fright wig.

"Wait, you're a pregnant octogenarian?" he asks.

"It's sort of like the Immaculate Conception," Donna says. "Or, what was that story in the Old Testament? That old woman who gets pregnant in her nineties? That's me. A nonagenarian. The miracle. The one who survives all trauma and tragedy."

Donna is also smoking a cigarette which somehow makes her fake pregnancy seem more authentic to him.

"I kind of like the idea of Cassie getting pregnant later in life. It works, doesn't it? I mean, Cassie does everything too late." Michael feels wise. Donna nods in agreement. Since the character of Cassie is based on Donna herself, her nodding feels both true and kind of heartbreaking.

"Oh, Michael." Donna stares off at the stage through the lobby door where some members of the party are already forming a drunken circle downstage right. "Do you remember how we used to stay up all night drinking after doing a show and then go and sober up in the morning by looking at Pollock's *Autumn Rhythm* at the Met?" Donna asks.

"Of course, I do, babe," he answers. Donna walks through the door leading up to the stage.

Once, during a workshop of the show at the Public, the actress Marsha Mason gave Michael some advice about the ending after watching a rehearsal performance. "You can't tell us we don't get a second chance," she said to him after she saw that Cassie doesn't make the final cut and has to leave the chorus line at the end of the show. "Cassie can't go through that whole catharsis and then not get the part. You just can't *do* that, Michael," she'd said to him. She was very upset about it.

That's why Cassie gets chosen for the chorus at the end of the show now. Cassie is the audience favorite after all. They're so invested in her—she just has to be chosen at the end. Marsha was speaking as an actor, of course, and actors always want to be chosen. But what she hit on is one of the things that is so true and so right—everyone wishes they could have a second chance at something. Michael wishes he could give Ernie a second chance.

"You get over here, Michael Bennett!" says Donna. "We're all going to do the finale up on the old stage!"

Acknowledgments

I'd like to thank the following people who all contributed to the writing of this book in some meaningful way: Carla Nassy, Emily Voorhees, Megan Byrne, Meaghan Bouchoux, Deb Bouchoux, Kathleen Rawson, Tom Doolittle, Anne Marie Morris, Christin Staples, Rick Somers, William F.A. Thompson, Jr. (AKA "Porky Motown Brooks"), Jim Petosa, Susannah Larson, Sherry Sabol, Aaron Hamburger, Maureen Brady, Sally Bellerose, Michael Carroll, and Angela Palm.

In the course of my research, I found several books very helpful: *Natasha: The Biography of Natalie Wood* by Suzanne Finstad, *Goodbye Natalie, Goodbye Splendour* by Marti Rulli with Dennis Davern, *Elizabeth Taylor: The Last Star* by Kitty Kelley, *A Hell of a Life: An Autobiography* by Maureen Stapleton and Jane Scovell, *A Chorus Line and the Musicals of Michael Bennett* by Ken Mandelbaum, and *One Singular Sensation: The Michael Bennett Story* by Kevin Kelly.

Special thanks to Raymond Luczak for his faith in this story series and for his patience and guidance during its publication.

About the Author

Philip Dean Walker holds a B.A. in American Literature from Middlebury College and an M.F.A. in Creative Writing from American University. His first book, *At Danceteria and Other Stories*, was named a *Kirkus Reviews* Best Book of 2017. His second book, *Read by Strangers*, was named a *Kirkus Reviews* Best Book of 2018. He lives in Washington, D.C.

philipdeanwalker.com

CPSIA information can be obtained
at www.ICGtesting.com
Printed in the USA
LVHW092331150921
697901LV00002B/98

9 781941 960158